My Shadow

Robert Louis Stevenson

Illustrations by Glenna Lang

David R. Godine · Publisher · Boston

First edition published in 1989 by
David R. Godine, Publisher, Inc.
Horticultural Hall
300 Massachusetts Avenue
Boston, Massachusetts 02115

Library of Congress Cataloging-in-Publication Data

Stevenson, Robert Louis, 1850–1894.
My shadow / by Robert Louis Stevenson : illustrated by Glenna Lang.
p. cm
Summary: An illustrated version of Stevenson's popular poem in
which a child tells about her relationship with her shadow.
ISBN 0-87923-788-0
1. Shades and shadows—Juvenile poetry. 2. Children's poetry,
Scottish. [1. Shadows—Poetry. 2. Scottish poetry.] I. Lang,
Glenna, ill. II. Title.
PR5489.S5 1989
821'.8—dc19   88-46107
CIP
AC

First printing
Printed in Hong Kong

My Shadow

For Esmé

I have a little shadow that goes in and out with me,

And what can be the use of him is more than I can see.

He is very, very like me from the heels up to the head;

And I see him jump before me,

when I jump into my bed.

The funniest thing about him

is the way he likes to grow—

Not at all like proper children,

which is always rather slow;

For he sometimes shoots up taller,

like an india-rubber ball,

And he sometimes gets so little

that there's none of him at all.

He hasn't got a notion of how children ought to play,

And can only make a fool of me in every sort of way.

He stays so close beside me,

he's a coward you can see;

I'd think shame to stick to nursie

as that shadow sticks to me!

One morning, very early,

before the sun was up,

I rose and found the shining dew on every buttercup;

But my lazy little shadow, like an arrant sleepy-head,

Had stayed at home behind me and was fast asleep in bed.